Thanksgiving

by Laura Alden
illustrated by Susan Lexa

created by Wing Park Publishers

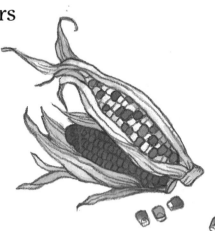

 CHILDRENS PRESS ®

CHICAGO

Note to Teacher or Parent:

The Thanksgiving tradition of placing five kernels of corn beside each plate and naming five blessings actually began in the late 1850's. The custom is based on the legend that during the "starving time" of 1623, the Pilgrims' ration of food dwindled to five kernels of corn a day for each person. While it is true that food was rationed during this time and that the Pilgrims celebrated the crop-saving rains with a Thanksgiving feast that year, the "five kernels" tradition remains a popular, rather than an historical tradition. It is practiced by members of The General Society of Mayflower Descendents who place five kernels of corn in scallop shells next to their Thanksgiving place settings each year. They each name five blessings at the beginning of their feast in memory of the hardship endured by the Pilgrims and in celebration of the abundance of our lives today.

Library of Congress Cataloging-in-Publication Data

Alden, Laura, 1955-
    Thanksgiving / by Laura Alden ; illustrated by Susan Lexa.
        p.   cm. — (Circle the year with holidays)
    "Created by Wing Park Publishers."
    Summary: Andrew, Abigail, and Elizabeth help prepare for their Thanksgiving dinner, share the story of the first Thanksgiving, and name the things for which they are thankful. Includes crafts, games, and activities.
    ISBN 0-516-00688-6
    [1. Thanksgiving Day—Fiction.]   I. Lexa-Senning, Susan, ill. II. Title. III. Series.
PZ7.A3586Th   1993
[E]—dc20   93-13019
                                                                   CIP
                                                                   AC

It was the Saturday before Thanksgiving. There was lots to do, because Grandma and Grandpa were coming for Thanksgiving Day.

3

Andrew, Abigail and Elizabeth were excited
when the family sat down for breakfast.

"Holidays are a lot more fun when we all
help prepare for them," said Mother. "There

are things we need to think about and things
we need to do."

"Right!" said Dad. "So let's make plans now."

"Well, I've filled this fat china turkey with notes for the 'Take Your Turn' game," said Mom. "I thought each of you could draw three notes from it."

"And," said Dad, "you have between now and Thursday to do the three things."

"Sounds like fun!" said Andrew. "Can I go first?"

"Sure," everyone said.

Andrew reached into the jar. "Make Thanksgiving placemats," he read. "Not too bad." Next
he drew, "Vacuum the house." "Still not too
bad," he said.

Andrew's third note said, "Read the story
of Thanksgiving and tell it to someone." "Yes!"
he shouted. "No dusting!"

Elizabeth drew, "Play 'Pin the Tailfeathers on the Turkey' with two other people." Next she read, "Make apple turkeys." Her last job was, "Dust the house."

"Ha!" said Andrew.

"Ha yourself," said Elizabeth. "I like dusting."

"Take your turn, Abigail," said Mom.

Abigail drew, "Paint your face with Indian symbols." "Grind cranberries," was next. Then Abigail drew, "On Thanksgiving Day, put five kernels of corn beside each plate."

"What's the corn for?" she asked.

"Well," said Mom, "one year the Pilgrims' crops didn't get enough rain. The Pilgrims didn't have much food to eat—maybe just a few grains of corn a day. Then rain came and their crops were saved."

"But why am I supposed to put corn by our plates?" asked Abigail.

"Many people use five kernels of corn to remember that the Pilgrims didn't have very much," Mom answered. "It also helps people remember how much we have today. So right before Thanksgiving dinner, we will each name five things for which we are thankful," said Mom.

"All right," said Elizabeth and Andrew together.

"Hmmmm...," said Abigail.

During the next few days, Abigail thought about what she should say when she picked up her corn. I'm thankful for special things, she thought, things such as books...games ...toys. But there must be other things, more special things for which I should be thankful.

On Thanksgiving morning, Abigail painted her face like an Indian's. She put the five kernels of corn beside each plate. Again she wondered what she should say at mealtime. Maybe she would tell how thankful she was for food or her house or her room. Still she wanted to think of something more special.

She found Elizabeth making turkeys out of apples and raisins. "What are you going to be thankful for?" Abigail asked her.

"Raisins for one thing," said Elizabeth, popping one in her mouth. "Want one?"

"Okay," said Abigail. "Now, let's go ask Andrew what he's going to be thankful for."

But Andrew was reading the story of the first Thanksgiving. "Did you know the Pilgrims came to America on a ship called the Mayflower?" he asked. "And the Indians, who lived here first, helped them get settled?"

Andrew showed them some pictures. "The
Pilgrims invited the Indians to a feast to help
celebrate their first harvest. That was the first
Thanksgiving."

"Time for cranberries!" called Mom. "I need
my best grinder."

Abigail ran to the kitchen. The cranberries
popped as she cranked the grinder.

"Hello!" shouted a voice. Abigail jumped.
Grandpa and Grandma had arrived.

"Mmmmm . . . pies!" said Andrew, helping Grandma set them down.

"Pumpkin, just as you all love," said Grandma.

"And a Thanksgiving Day hug, one for each
of you," said Grandpa.

Soon it was time for dinner. Everyone gathered around the table. Suddenly Abigail remembered the corn by her plate. She still wasn't sure what five things she was going to say.

Grandpa picked up his five kernels. "I'm thankful for peace, for freedom, for health, for

the beautiful day, and for all of this food!" he
said.

Abigail stared at her corn. She hardly heard
the others speak. *What should she say?*

"Abigail," said Mom softly. "What are you
thankful for?"

It was her turn. Abigail looked up at Mom and Dad and at Grandma. They were smiling at her. She looked at Grandpa and Andrew and Elizabeth. They smiled too. And at last Abigail knew what she was going to say.

One by one, she picked up her pieces of corn.

"Number 1," she said, "I'm thankful for my parents. Number 2, I'm thankful for my grandparents. Number 3, I'm thankful for you, Andrew. Number 4, I'm thankful for you, Elizabeth. And Number 5, or last of all, I'm

thankful for this home where all of us love
one another. Yes, I'm very thankful on this
Thanksgiving Day."

"Beautiful," said Mom. "And now, please
pass the turkey."

Thanksgiving Fun with Learning

At your family or school Thanksgiving feast, use the "five kernels" custom of giving thanks. Here are some additional ways to celebrate Thanksgiving.

1. Things to Create

Make apple turkeys—and eat them! Have available an apple, a small box of raisins, one green olive with pimento and five toothpicks for each child. Have children thread raisins onto toothpicks for turkey feathers. Place apple on its side; stick feathers into one end of apple. Stick olive on toothpick for head and poke into other end of apple.

Thanksgiving for birds.

Locate a large pinecone and a pipe cleaner for each child. Have available jars of peanut butter and some wild bird seed. Spread pinecone with peanut butter; then roll in bird seed. Attach pipe cleaner to feeder for hanging in a tree.

Create a thank you collage—on placemats or bulletin board. Have children help gather photographs, clippings and drawings of people, places and things for which they are thankful. Tape or glue pieces onto white placemats or tack onto bulletin board. Lettering could read, "We Are Thankful For..." or "I Am Thankful For..."

2. Thing to Do

Play "Hide the Indian Corn" (allowing children to take turns hiding the corn around the room while a rotating team of finders waits outside). Also try "Harvest Basket Upset," a variation on "Fruit Basket Upset," using corn, gourds, pumpkins, squash, nuts, etc. "Pin the Tailfeathers on the Turkey" and "Duck, Duck, Goose" are other seasonal favorites.

Teach children basic folk or square dance steps to use as part of their Thanksgiving day celebration. Pair Indians with Pilgrims and dance to traditional folk music ("Turkey in the Straw," etc.)

3. Things to Count, Sort and Match

Practice sorting, counting, and classifying by having children "set the table" for a class or family Thanksgiving feast. Use paper or plastic dishes, cups and utensils.

Create a sequencing and storytelling activity by providing picture cards with simple Indian symbols (an inverted **v** for a mountain, circle for the sun, etc.).

4. Things to Share

In addition to the always popular "Over the River and Through the Woods," learn one or more of the following songs and fingerplays:

Funny Turkey

A turkey is a funny bird,
Its head goes wobble, wobble,
   *(move head from side to
   side)*
It knows just one funny word—
"Gobble, gobble, gobble!"
   (shouted)

We Are Pilgrims, We Are Indians

(Sung to the tune of Frere Jacques)

We are Pilgrims. We are
   Indians.
Yes we are. Yes we are.
We will eat together. We
   will eat together.
Let's be friends. Let's be
   friends.
      —Laura Alden

Thanksgiving Friends

To see what he could see,
   (hand over eyes)
A little Indian climbed a
   tree.
   (walk fingers up left arm)
A little Pilgrim climbed one
   too.
   (walk fingers up right arm)
Asked the Pilgrim, "Who are
   you?"
   (point out with finger)
The Indian raised his hand
   to send
The Indian sign for friend.
   *(put index and middle fingers
   up—Indian sign language
   for friend)*